A GOLDEN BOOK • NEW YORK

A Skipping Day

Adapted by Andrea Posner-Sanchez

Story concept by Tea Orsi

Illustrated by Stefania Fiorillo,
Raffaella Seccia, and Gianluca Barone

I't's a nice day on Shipwreck Beach. Jake and his crew are playing with a jump rope.

"Yay, hey! This jump rope is fun!" Izzy says.

"It's awesome!" Jake agrees.

Skully flutters this way and that way, happily flying under the rope when he gets a chance.

Jake, Izzy, and Skully don't know it, but Captain Hook is spying on them with his spyglass.

"Those puny pirates are having fun with that jumpy thing," says Hook. "I want to have fun, too!"

"I must have that jumpy thing," Captain Hook tells his first mate, Mr. Smee. "Get me that treasure!" Mr. Smee salutes Hook and says, "Yes, Cap'n!"

Meanwhile, back on the beach, the pirate crew is ready for a healthy snack.

"It's smoothie time, mateys!" announces Cubby.

"Thanks, Cubby," says Izzy. "All that jumping has made me thirsty."

"Those look great, Cubby!" says Jake.
Jake puts the jump rope on the sand. After he and his friends drink their smoothies, they will jump some more.

Jake, Izzy, and Skully head over to Cubby.
"Crackers! I love smoothies!" says Skully.

As the pirates enjoy their drinks, Captain Hook and Smee sneak onto the beach. "The jumpy thing is mine, Smee!" Hook declares.

Skully spots the scoundrels.
"It's Captain Hook!" he cries.
Jake turns just in time to see
Hook and Smee running away.

"Hey! He stole our jump rope!"
Izzy says as Captain Hook and
Smee head into Tiki Tree Forest.
"Yo, ho! Let's get our treasure
back!" declares Jake.

The pirate crew rushes to catch up with Hook and Smee. Unfortunately, a river stops them in their tracks.

"Aw, coconuts! How did Hook and Smee get to the other side of this river?" Cubby asks.

Izzy thinks for a moment. Then she comes up with a solution.
"We'll jump on the stones to cross the river," she says.
Jake thinks it's a great idea. "Yo, ho! Way to go!"

"Let's do it on the count of three," says Izzy. "One, two, three!"

Jake, Izzy, and Cubby jump on the rocks and cross the river. Skully cheers them on. "Crackers! You're doing it!" calls the parrot.

Everyone is having fun. "I love jumping!" exclaims Cubby.

When they reach the other side of the
river, Jake and his crew quickly catch up to
Captain Hook and Mr. Smee.

"Please give us back our jump rope,
Captain Hook!" cries Jake.
   "Never!" Captain Hook says. "It's
my turn to have fun!"

Hook is all set to finally play with the jump rope.
Izzy notices that the rope is tangled around his feet.
"Watch out, Hook!" Izzy warns.

But Captain Hook doesn't listen.
He falls to the ground, all tied up.
"Smee!" Hook cries. "Save meee!"

Izzy and Jake rush over to help. In no time, the
friends free Captain Hook from the jump rope.

"Barnacles! That jumpy thing is broken," Captain Hook declares. "I don't want it anymore."

"It's not broken," Jake says, smiling.

"We'll teach you how to use it," Izzy adds.

The jolly buccaneers show Captain Hook and Smee what to do. Before long, they're all jumping—and having fun!

"I'm jumping, Smee! I'm jumping!" shouts Hook happily.

"Well done, Cap'n," says Smee.

The Pirate Games

Adapted by Andrea Posner-Sanchez

Story concept by Alessandro Sisti

Illustrated by Stefania Fiorillo,
Roberta Zanotta,
and Giuseppe Fontana

It's an exciting day on Pirate Island. Jake, Izzy, and Cubby are going to compete against Captain Hook's crew in the Never Land Pirate Games.

The team that wins gets a special treasure—a golden pirate trophy!

"Smee! I want that golden trophy thing!" Hook yells to his first mate.

The first event is the rope climb. "You have to climb to the top and ring the bell," explains Jake.

Izzy will climb for Jake's team. She loves climbing.

Hook orders Bones to do the climbing
for his team. But Bones is afraid of heights.

Izzy and Bones stand by their ropes. Jake starts the competition by calling out, "Ready? Yo, ho! Let's go!"

Izzy uses all her strength to pull herself up the rope. "I'm going to make it to the top," she tells herself as her teammates cheer her on.

Bones is barely off the ground. "It's scary, Cap'n!" he says to Hook.

Before long, Izzy reaches
the platform and rings the bell.
"Izzy wins!" cries Skully.

Captain Hook isn't happy. "Barnacles!" he hollers at Bones, who is all tangled up in his rope. "I'm not going to get the trophy like that!"

Now it's time for
the water cannon
target event. Cubby is
going first. He aims his
cannon, and . . .

SPLASH! Cubby knocks down the target.
"Bull's-eye!"cries Skully.

Next it's Smee's turn. He is trying to concentrate, but his teammates are making him nervous.

"Hit it here," Sharky calls out as he
and Bones jump around the target.
"You better not miss!" Hook yells,
and then glares at Smee.

Smee closes his eyes and squirts his water cannon. "Did I hit the target?" he asks.

"No, Smee!" hollers Hook as he gets knocked over by the stream of water. "I am not the target!"

For the last event, the teams head to an old pirate ship on the edge of the beach. "This is the pirate balance challenge," Cubby tells everyone.

"You have to walk across the ship's mast without falling."

Hook decides he will do this event himself.

But first it is Jake's turn. He holds his arms out to the sides, looks straight ahead, and carefully walks across the mast.

"Way to go, Jake!" cheers Cubby.
"Yay, hey! You did it!" yells Izzy.

"Bah! I can keep my balance, too," says Hook as he stands on the mast. The captain takes a few steps and starts to wobble.

Then the wobbling turns into falling!
"Help me, Smee!" cries Hook.

Once Captain Hook is fished out of the water, Jake and his crew begin to celebrate their win.

"Oh, dear, Cap'n," says Smee. "It looks like we lost."

"And I really wanted that golden trophy thing," Hook whines.

Jake, Izzy, and Cubby are proud of themselves. They worked well as a team and won the Never Land Pirate Games! Maybe they'll even let Hook borrow their trophy one day. . . .

SHADOW PLAY!

Adapted by Andrea Posner-Sanchez

Story concept by Silvia Lombardi

Illustrated by Gianluca Panniello and Giuseppe Fontana

One evening, Jake, Izzy, and Cubby are walking along the beach as the sun begins to go down.

"Cool sunset!" Izzy says as she points toward the horizon.

Skully the parrot agrees. "Look at the cool colors!" he squawks.

Soon the pirates stop in their
tracks. A huge, scary shadow lies
in front of them. "That looks like
a m-m-monster!" Cubby says
nervously.

"Watch out, gang," Jake warns
as he turns around to investigate.

Izzy notices that the shadow changes when Jake moves. "There's no monster," she says with a giggle. "*We're* making that scary shadow!"

"Whew!" sighs Skully.

Everyone laughs.

"Hey," adds Cubby, "this gives me an idea."

Cubby leads the crew to a large rock.
He entertains his friends by making
shadow puppets with his hands.
"That one looks like a rabbit," says Izzy.
"Great job, Cubby," Jake tells him.

Meanwhile, back at the *Jolly Roger*, Mr. Smee is trying to entertain Captain Hook with a puppet show. "I'm the great Captain Hook, and I'm going to get you, Mr. Crocodile, sir," Smee says as he makes the sock puppet talk.

Captain Hook just yawns. "I'm bored, Smee," he announces.

Just then, Hook spots Jake and his crew through
his spyglass. "Barnacles!" he shouts. "Those puny
pirates have found a treasure. I've got to have it!"
He and Smee hop in their dinghy and row to shore.

Captain Hook doesn't realize it's not a real treasure—Jake and his crew are making a shadow in the shape of a treasure chest!

"Cool!" Izzy declares as she and her friends stand in the perfect positions to make the shadow. "This looks real!"

By the time Hook and Smee get to the beach, the kids are making a different shadow. This one scares the greedy pirate.

"Smee, the crocodile is here!" Captain Hook cries. "Hide!"

Hook trembles in fear as Jake and his friends admire their shadow. "It looks just like Tick Tock Croc!" says Jake.

"It's awesome!" Cubby shouts.

"It's just a shadow the sea pups made," Smee tells the captain.

But Captain Hook doesn't believe him. "No, it's the crocodile!" he shouts from his hiding place.

"Really," Jake admits. "It's just us."

Jake, Izzy, and Cubby make another shadow to show Hook there's nothing to worry about.
"Look, Cap'n," says Smee. "The crocodile is gone and now it's a treasure chest."

Captain Hook comes out to peek. "Well, where is the treasure?" he demands.

"There's no treasure," Smee explains. "The little pirates are making funny shadows."

Jake invites Captain Hook to make shadows with them. "Oh, please can we join them?" Smee begs.

But Hook shakes his head. "I don't like silly shadows. Back to the *Jolly Roger*," he orders.

As Hook and Smee get in their dinghy, the kids continue having fun with shadows.

"Guess what I'm making now," says Cubby as he kneels and holds his arms over his head.

The friends take a look
and smile.

"Crackers!" squawks
Skully. "It's a coconut!"

"Or a bowling ball,"
suggests Izzy.

"Good one, Cubby!"
says Jake.

Captain Hook and Smee are halfway back to the *Jolly Roger* when they spot a familiar-looking shadow in the water.

But Hook isn't worried. "It's just those puny pirates doing more shadow tricks," he says confidently.

Tick tock. Tick tock.
  It really is the crocodile this time! Hook jumps into Smee's arms. "Save me, Smee!" he cries.

"Paddle, Smee! Paddle!" Captain Hook orders.
The nervous pirates make it to the *Jolly Roger*
safe and sound. "Now I don't like crocodiles *and*
shadows!" Hook yells as the sun finishes setting.